DC SUPER HERO GIRLS™

HARLEY QUINN'S BRAIN-SQUEEZERS!

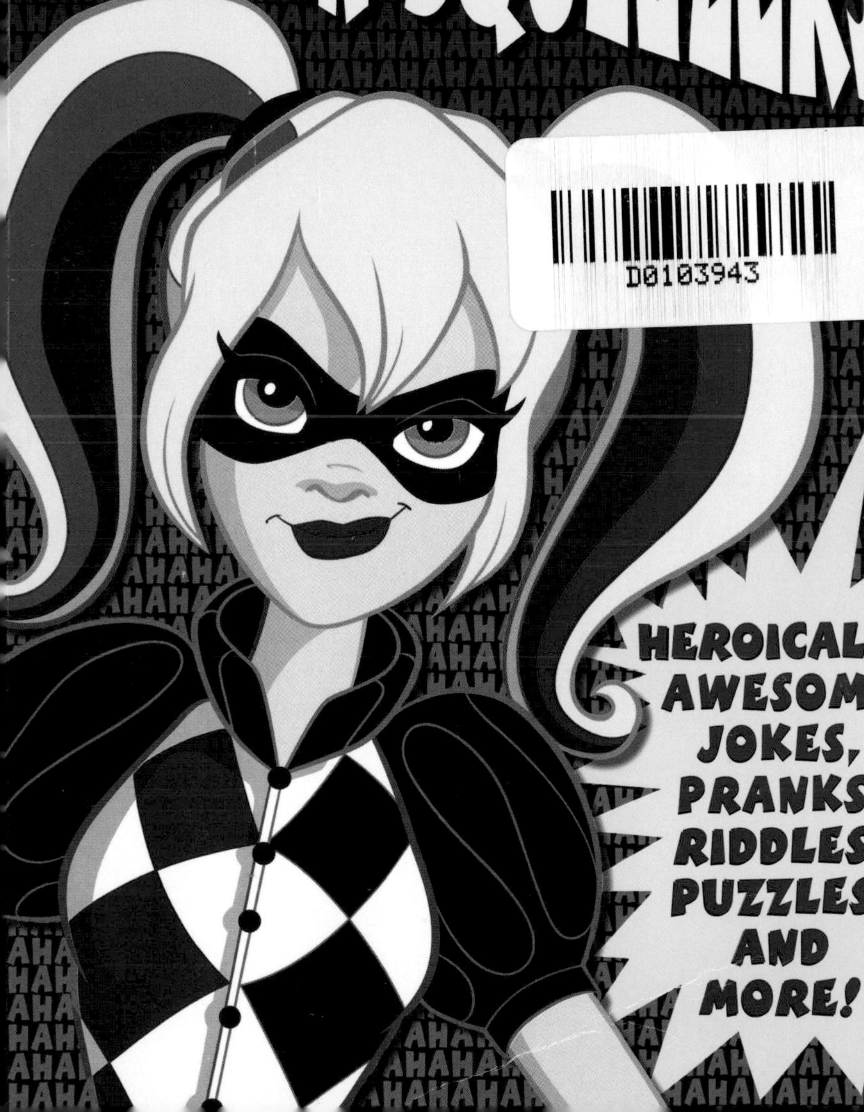

HEROICALLY AWESOME JOKES, PRANKS, RIDDLES, PUZZLES, AND MORE!

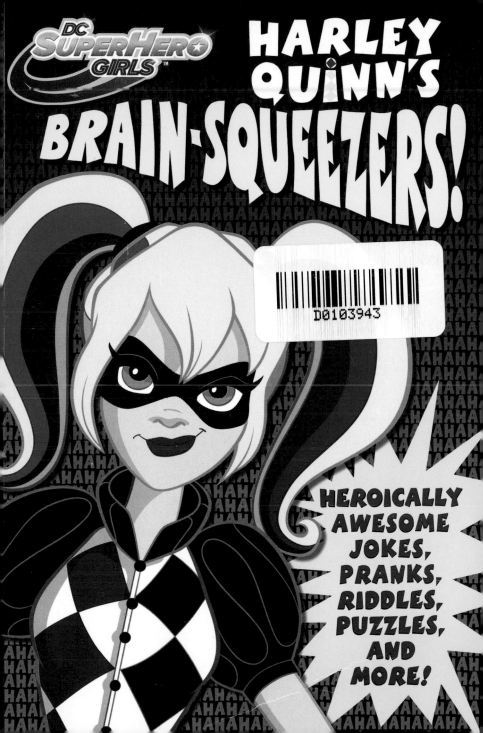

US $5.99/ $7.99 CAN

ISBN 978-1-5247-6395-4

9 781524 763954

5 0 5 9 9

HARLEY QUINN'S BRAIN-SQUEEZERS!

By C. Lee

Additional illustrations by Francesco Legramandi

Random House 🏠 New York

Copyright © 2017 DC Comics.
DC SUPER HERO GIRLS and all related characters and elements
© & ™ DC Comics and Warner Bros. Entertainment Inc.
WB SHIELD: ™ & © WBEI. (s17)
RHUS39300
All Rights Reserved. Published in the United States by Random House Children's Books,
a division of Penguin Random House LLC, 1745 Broadway, New York, NY 10019, and
in Canada by Penguin Random House Canada Limited, Toronto. Random House and
the colophon are registered trademarks of Penguin Random House LLC.
randomhousekids.com
dcsuperherogirls.com
dckids.com
ISBN 978-1-5247-6395-4 (trade)
Printed in the United States of America
10 9 8 7 6 5 4 3 2 1

WELCOME TO SUPER HERO HIGH!

Hiya, friends!

WELCOME TO SUPER HERO HIGH SCHOOL. It's not your usual academic institution. Besides studyin' history, math, and all the other usual stuff, the students here train to become super heroes. And we're all uniquely qualified. Some of us fly, shrink, freeze, turn invisible, or use otherworldly hocus-pocus. Others are aliens with strange powers, while some just have plain ol' can-do brute super-strength. And the techie ones use gadgets to make themselves *totally* super.

Me? I think it's my unique perspective that makes me super. I laugh in the face of danger. Well . . . come to think of it, I laugh most of the time.

I'm Harley Quinn—jokester extraordinaire, comedy genius, the funniest, punniest pigtailed prankster around. Nobody's better at tellin' jokes than yours truly. And there's no better way to save Metropolis from crooks, criminals, and villains than with an expertly delivered *punch* line.

KA-BOOM!

Think you got what it takes to break codes, solve riddles, and outsmart super-villains? Get your cape on, pull your thinkin' cap down over your noggin, and see if you can figure out my zaniest, craziest brain-squeezers!

Use the key to reveal the secret message.

$$\overline{}\ \overline{}\ \overline{}\ \overline{}\ \overline{}\ \overline{}\ \overline{}\ \overline{}$$
6   2   13   24   2   5   17   25

$$\overline{}\ \overline{}\ \overline{}$$
1   23   24

$$\overline{}\ \overline{}\ \overline{}\ \overline{}\ \overline{}\ \overline{}$$
21   2   24   23   15   14

$$\overline{}\ \overline{}\ \overline{}\ \overline{}\ \overline{}\ \overline{}!$$
9   5   10   6   21   22

$$\overline{}\ \overline{}-\overline{}\ \overline{}!$$
21   5   21   5

1 = F	8 = W	15 = I	22 = S
2 = E	9 = L	16 = V	23 = O
3 = M	10 = U	17 = D	24 = R
4 = Q	11 = J	18 = Z	25 = Y
5 = A	12 = K	19 = E	26 = B
6 = G	13 = T	20 = X	
7 = N	14 = C	21 = H	

ANSWER: Get ready for heroic laughs! Ha-ha!

JOKE BREAK

Why did Wonder Woman wrap herself in aluminum?

She wanted to *foil* crime.

Why do super heroes love calendars?

They're always saving the day!

How do you know Harley Quinn is running for school president?

She put her name on the *mallet*!

How did Catwoman fail her Weaponomics midterm?

She really *bombed* the test.

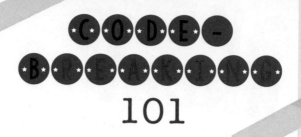

CODE-BREAKING 101

Every good super hero needs to be a super-smart sleuth. That's why we learn all about cryptography at Super Hero High School. Your mission, if you choose to accept it, is to use your detective skills to crack the code.

Hint: Circle every second letter to reveal the secret message.

A	M	R	E	U	E	T	T	W	M	G
	E	P	A	H	T	O	C	S	A	
M	P	I	E	K	S	L	A	C	N	X
	D	B	C	E	O	J	W	Z	L	
B	S	V	C	D	A	N	F	Q	E	F

Lois Lane Reports:
Cryptography is the science of creating—and deciphering—secret communications.

ANSWER: Meet me at Capes and Cowls Café.

KNOCKOUTS!

 Knock-knock.

Who's there?

Lettuce.

Lettuce who?

Lettuce order, Steve!
I'm starving!

 Knock-knock.

Who's there?

Donut.

Donut who?

Donut forget to tip
your waiter!

Welcome to
CAPES & COWLS CAFÉ

Nothing beats Capes & Cowls when you're in the mood for an after-school snack!

What's Katana's favorite thing to order?

Pizza by the slice.

8

How do super heroes prefer to quench their thirst?

Fruit *punch*!

What happened to Captain Cold when he got a job at Capes & Cowls?

He became a smoothie operator.

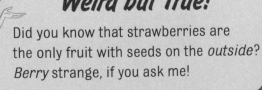

Weird but True!

Did you know that strawberries are the only fruit with seeds on the *outside*? *Berry* strange, if you ask me!

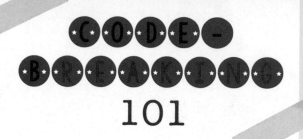

CODE-BREAKING 101

Listen up, Harley fans: I'm always on the lookout for the most excellent, most exciting, most electrifying info to share with loyal viewers of *Harley's Quinntessentials*. And guess what? Someone at Capes & Cowls Café just slipped me this note. . . .

Well, what are you waitin' for, an engraved invitation? Use the cipher to decode the message. It might be some exclusive news I can feature on my vlog!

Hint: Replace each letter in the message with the letter above or below it in the cipher.

QBAG BEQRE GUR PYBJA OHETRE.

VG GNFGRF SHAAL!

A B C D E F G H I J K L M
↕ ↕ ↕ ↕ ↕ ↕ ↕ ↕ ↕ ↕ ↕ ↕ ↕
N O P Q R S T U V W X Y Z

ANSWER: Don't order the Clown Burger. It tastes funny!

Lois Lane Reports:

A *cipher* is a way to encode or decode secret communications.

JOKE BREAK

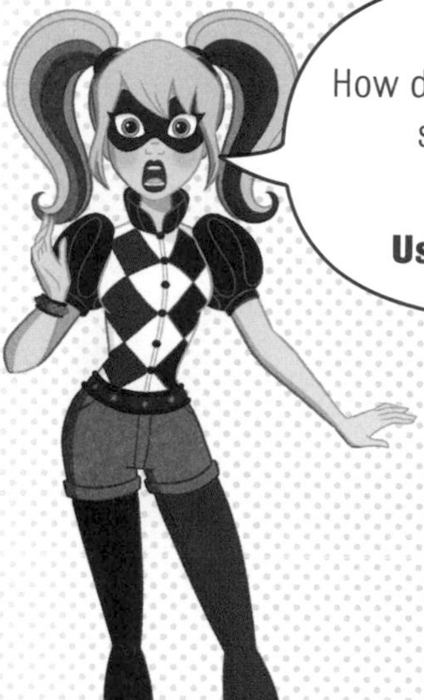

How do you keep a computer safe from robbers and criminals?

Use a screen saver.

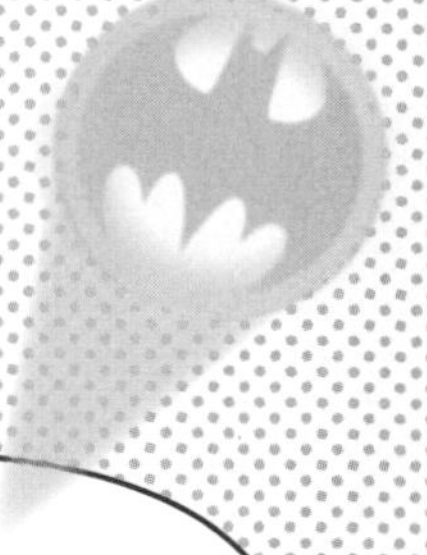

How does Batgirl let you know that she's going to make a left-hand turn?

She uses the Bat-Signal.

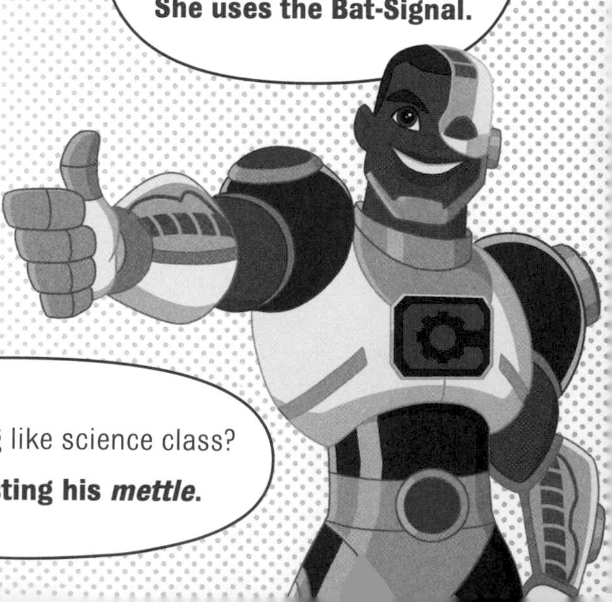

Why does Cyborg like science class?

He enjoys testing his *mettle*.

Weird but True!

Mettle means courage and determination, but it sounds an awful lot like *metal*—and Cyborg's got plenty of both! Words that sound the same but mean different things are called *homophones*.

When is Beast Boy not to be trusted?

When he's *a lion*.

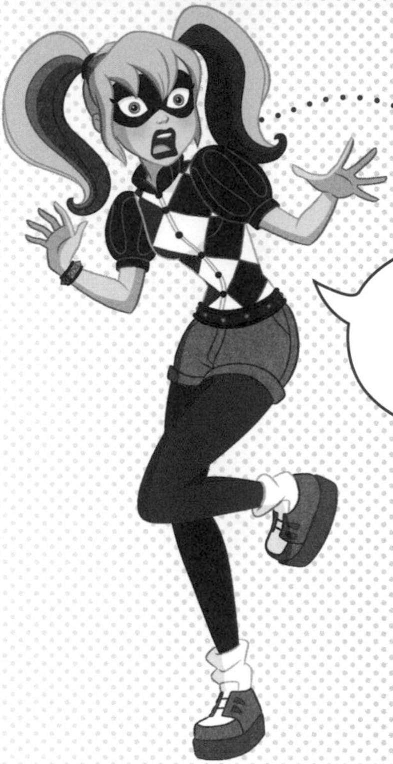

When is Elasti-Girl not to be trusted?

When she's *stretchin'* the truth.

How does Batgirl unwind after a long day of fighting crime?

She soaks in her *bat* tub.

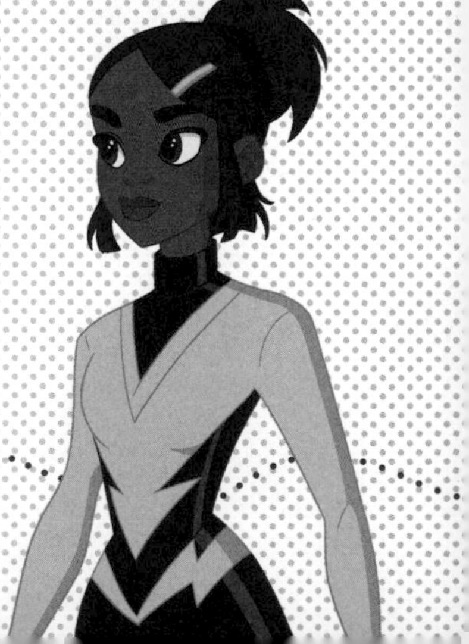

What does Thunder put on underneath her jumpsuit?

***Thunder* wear.**

What do you call a freshly shaved super-villain?

A smooth criminal.

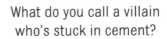

What do you call a villain who's stuck in cement?

A hardened criminal.

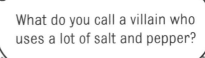

What do you call a villain who uses a lot of salt and pepper?

A seasoned criminal.

Pop Quiz #1: Super Hero Skills

Name _____   Date _____

Q: You're trapped in a room with a dangerous super-villain, and there are only two ways out: the window or the stairs. Which should you use to escape?

A: The window. You can never trust stairs. They're always up to something.

Q: What do villains use graph paper for?

A: Plotting their escape!

Rumor has it that a new teacher is comin' to Super Hero High, and a mysterious messenger claims to know who it is. This riddlin' rabble-rouser has promised to send us five clues to the teacher's identity. Here's the first one—help me figure it out, why don't you?

Dear Harley,

I am a seed that's small, round, and green.
In soups, stews, and side dishes is where
I'm usually seen.
What am I?

—A Friend in the Know

Pop Quiz #2: Super Hero Skills

Name _____ Date _____

Q: You're suiting up to save the day, and you can choose one super accessory: X-ray-vision goggles or antigravity boots. Which should you choose?

A: X-ray-vision goggles. Antigravity boots are impossible to put down.

Weird but True!

Did you know that flamingos only eat with their heads upside down? I bet they make excellent acrobats!

KNOCKOUTS!

 Knock-knock.

Who's there?

Stan.

Stan who?

Stan back while I toss this glitter bomb!

 Knock-knock.

Who's there?

Canoe.

Canoe who?

Canoe help me save the day?

JOKE BREAK

How do Supergirl and Starfire organize a trip to space?

They *planet*.

What did the super hero use to repair her costume?

Masking tape.

Hawkgirl and Bumblebee got into a disagreement. How was it?

It was *hawk*-ward.

Why is Supergirl such an incredible hero?

She's very *cape*-able.

Why is Cheetah so competitive?

She's *purr*-fectly willing to claw her way to the top.

JUSTICE for LAUGHS

What happened when Wonder Woman spent all night wonderin' how to save the day?

In the mornin', the answer *dawned* on her.

What did Crazy Quilt and his enemy do after a fight?

They patched things up.

Why was The Flash mad at Frost?

She gave him the cold shoulder.

How does Catwoman do her holiday shopping?

She uses a *cat*alog.

RIDDLE ME THIS

This just in: We've received a second clue. Can you help me guess the answer to this latest rhyme?

Dear Harley,

I'm curvy and sleek,
Though common as can be.
You'll find me between
Letter *R* and letter *T*.
What am I?

—A Friend in the Know

ANSWER: The letter S.

CAMPUS MAZE

Quick, you're late for class! Find your way through campus, avoiding the booby traps along the way.

JOKE BREAK

Why didn't Batgirl study
for her final exams?
She decided to wing it.

Why does Poison Ivy want
to fight crime?
**She's itching to save
the day.**

What did Catwoman say when she was named Hero of the Month?

"You've got to be *kitten* me."

What does Cheetah say when she's feeling discouraged?

"It's im-*paw*-sible!"

What do you call Bumblebee when she can't make up her mind?

A may-*bee*.

Tongue Twisters

Sometimes super heroes have to twist and turn out of some tight situations. Can you recite these tongue twisters without gettin' tongue-tied?

 This quick-witted queen of comedy makes villains quiver and quake with the quality of her quirky quips and puns.

 The jaunty jester juggled joyously while jiggling at his jokes.

 A big, bad burglar broke into the biscuit bakery before being bagged by Batgirl.

Now try recitin' them again, but this time do it standin' on your head!

For KICKS and GiGGLES

I was surprised when the clown held the door open for me.

It was a nice *jester*.

Why did the thief wear stripes?

He didn't want to be spotted.

Why does everyone like Poison Ivy?

She really grows on you.

CODE-BREAKING 101

Hey, wannabe world-savers! I hope you've been keepin' up with your cryptography lessons, because Batgirl just intercepted an encrypted message from some students at CAD Academy. Everybody knows this rival school is a trainin' ground for future super-villains and all-around bad eggs. But the joke's on them, because we're gonna use this cipher to crack their code!

A	B	C
D	E	F
G	H	I

J	K	L
M	N	O
P	Q	R

S · T · U · V

W · X · Y · Z

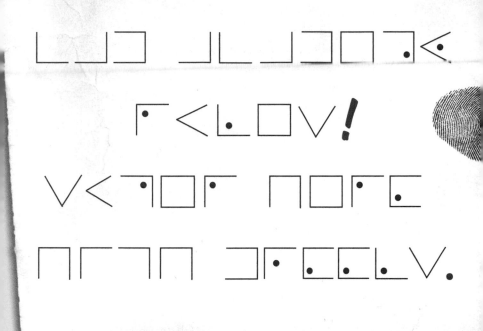

Hint: Each symbol corresponds to a letter in the grid.
Match the lines to reveal the letters.

Lois Lane Reports:
Encryption is the process of coding
messages to keep them secret.
To read an encrypted message, you
must use a cipher or a key.

JUSTICE for LAUGHS

Star Sapphire lost her power ring during an epic battle with a super-villain.

You mean the one that controls people's emotions?

Yeah. She's not sure how she feels about it.

Why wasn't Bumblebee surprised when she won Hero of the Month?

She had heard the *buzz*.

Why does Poison Ivy use insecticide on her plants?

Insects really *bug* her.

What does Catwoman say when she feels scared?

"That really freaked *meowt*!"

Pop Quiz #3: Super Hero Skills

Name _____ Date _____

Q: You're in the middle of an intense battle with Solomon Grundy. The only available weapon is a boomerang, but you've forgotten how to use it. What should you do?

A: Just throw it. It'll come back to you.

JOKE BREAK

Where does Poison Ivy
want to go to college?

Anywhere in the Ivy League.

What happens to Crazy Quilt
when it rains?

**He turns into a real
wet blanket.**

Harley-isms!

You know, I thought about replacin' Wonder Woman's bed with a trampoline, like mine.

But I was worried she'd hit the roof!

My website has never been more popular, but even so, I'm not feelin' well.

I think I've gone viral.

RIDDLE ME THIS

We're gettin' ever closer to discovering the identity of the newest teacher at Super Hero High. Can you solve the third clue?

Dear Harley,

Reporters ask questions,
Such as "Who?" "What?" and "When?"
They might even ask "Where?"
But what do they ask then?
        —A Friend in the Know

ANSWER: Why?

For KICKS and GIGGLES

Did you hear Commissioner Gordon arrested a villain who was robbin' the office supply store?

The bad guy was caught on tape.

Why did the super-villain use a sewin' machine?

He was following a pattern.

KNOCKOUTS!

 Knock-knock.

Who's there?

Accordion.

Accordion who?

Accordion to Mr. Fox,
we have a test next Friday.

 Knock-knock.

Who's there?

Frank.

Frank who?

Frank you for laughin'
at my jokes!

Pop Quiz #4: Super Hero Skills

Name _____ Date _____

Q: A super-villain is terrorizing the citizens of Metropolis at a local shopping mall. Your job is to neutralize the threat while keeping everyone calm. Should you fly up to the second floor or take the moving stairs?

A: Fly. Moving stairs tend to escalate quickly.

JUSTICE for LAUGHS

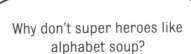

Why don't super heroes like alphabet soup?

Eatin' it could spell disaster.

Why does Lois Lane hang out at the ice cream shop?

To get the scoop.

Test Your Memory: Part 1

SUPERS-IN-TRAINING HAVE LOTS TO REMEMBER:
escape routes, code-breakin' skills, super hero history,
the location of their secret stash of whoopee cushions . . .

Oh, maybe that last one's just me. Ha-ha! Anyway, is
your memory in tip-top shape? Let's find out!

Take a second to study the cards on the opposite
page. Commit each face to memory, and pay close
attention to where each super hero—and super-villain—
is located.

	A	B	C	D
1	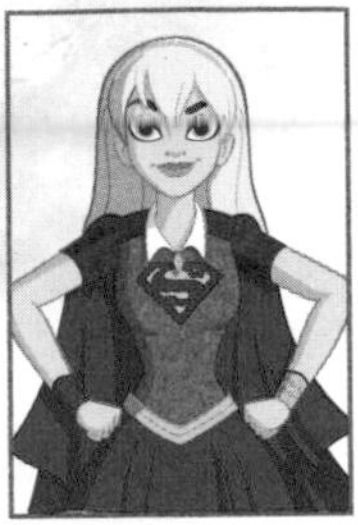	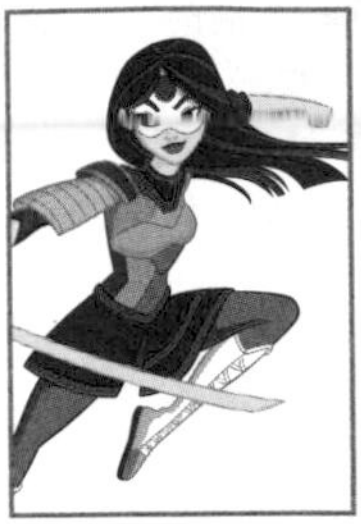	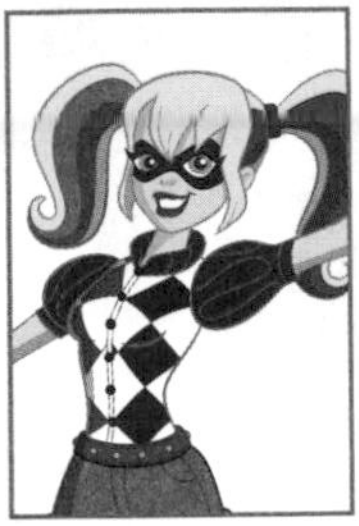	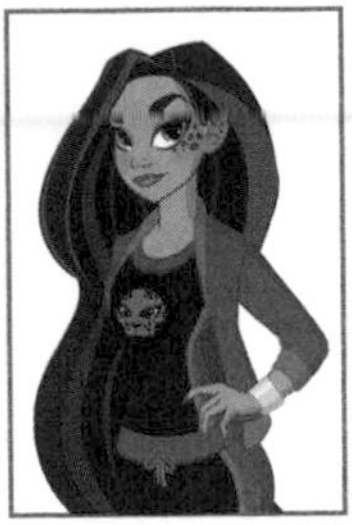
2	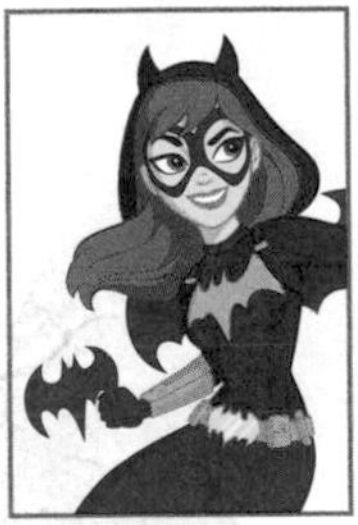	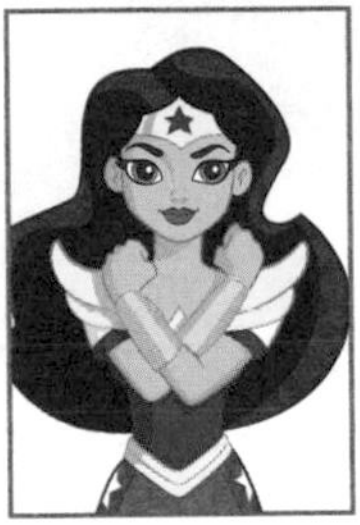	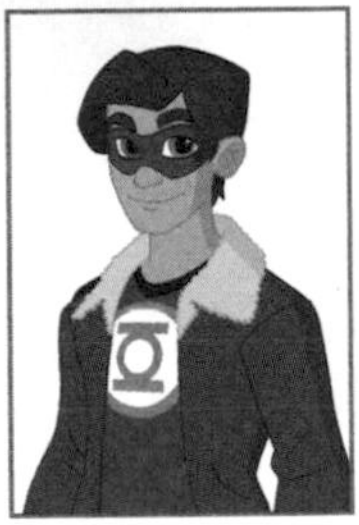	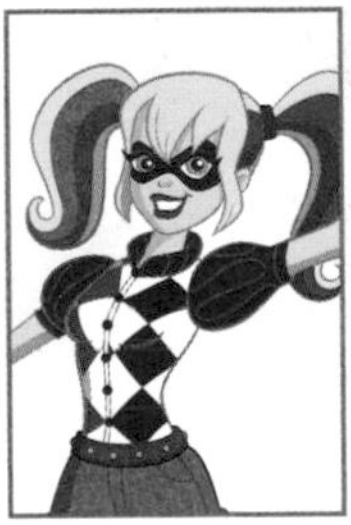
3	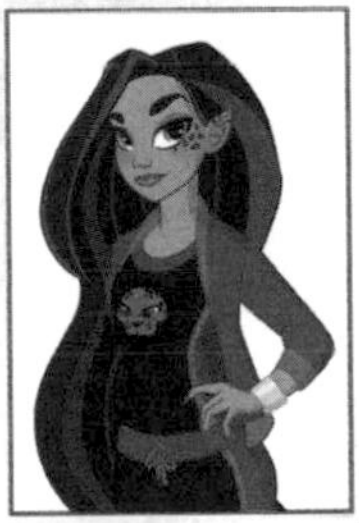	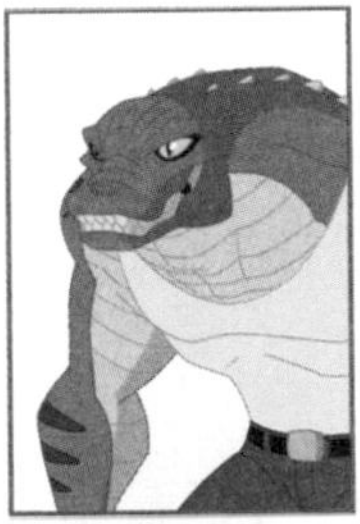	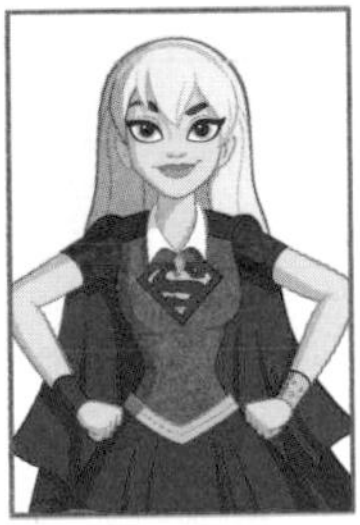	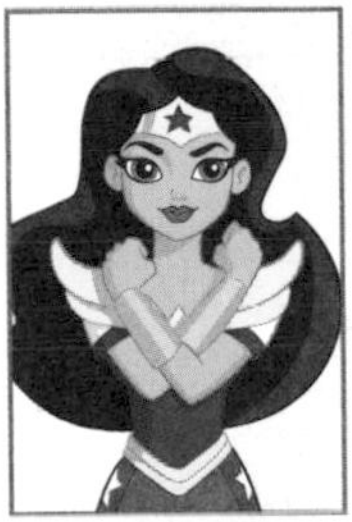
4	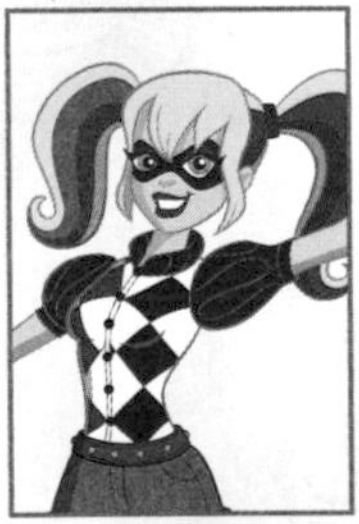	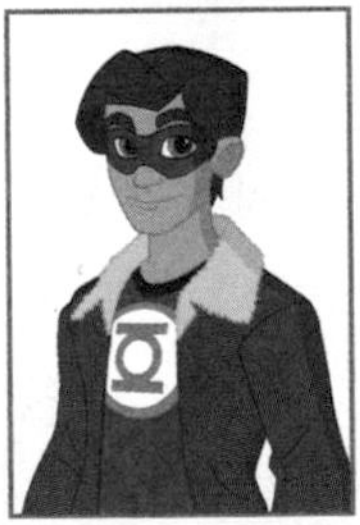	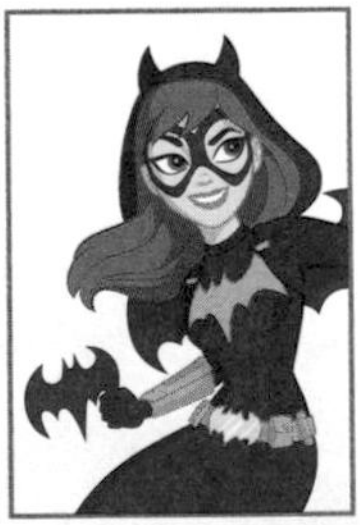	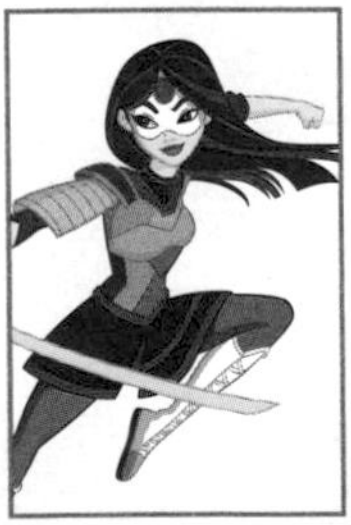

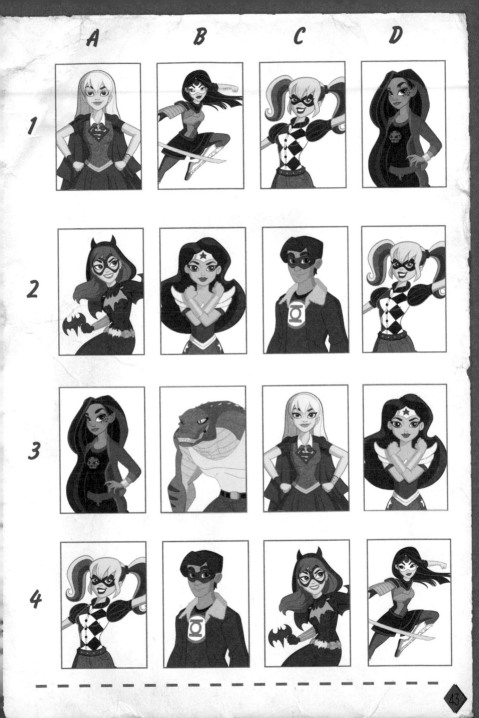

JOKE BREAK

What do you call The Flash when he's readin' the paper?

Newsflash.

How do you put a baby alien to sleep?

You *rocket*.

What do you call a rude super-villain who's falling through the air?

Condescending.

What's it called when a villain steals someone's coffee?

A *mugging*.

Why is the Green Lantern considered one of the most agreeable students at Super Hero High?

He's always giving his friends the green light.

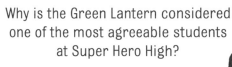

Pop Quiz #5: Super Hero Skills

Name _____ Date _____

Q: You're headed to Capes & Cowls Café, when suddenly you're attacked by a mob of angry clowns. What should you do?

A: Go for the juggler.

Q: Why should you never lie to someone with X-ray vision?

A: They can see right through you.

Food for Thought

What's The Flash's favorite food?

Fast food!

What happens when Vice Principal Grodd gets upset?

He goes bananas!

What's Frost's favorite part of the cake?

The icing!

Test Your Memory: Part 2

I HOPE YOU WERE PAYIN' ATTENTION! Can you remember where the evil super-villain Croc is lurkin'?

Having trouble? Maybe your photographic memory just hasn't *developed* yet. Do a backflip to page 43 and try again.

ANSWER: Row 3, Column B.

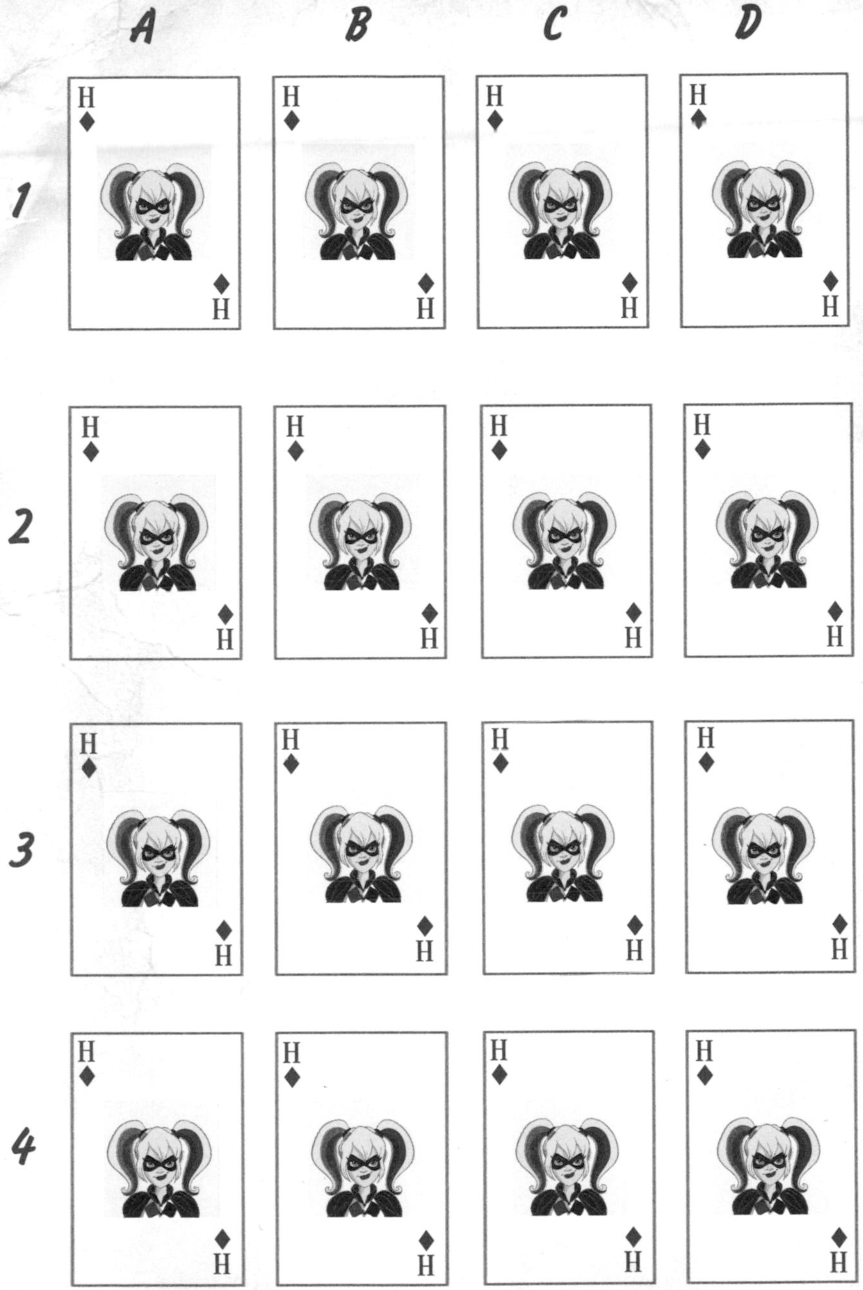
A
B
C
D
1
2
3
4

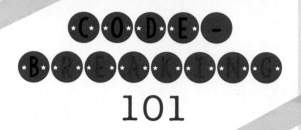

CODE-BREAKING 101

To translate the coded message below, use the key on the opposite page and write the letter corresponding to each symbol on the lines below.

___ , ___ ___ ___ ___

___ ___ ___ , ___ ___ ___ ___ ___ ___ ___ !

```
\   4  99  \  x  #
( )  !  K  &  22
:  K  $  22  &  !
```

% = A

ZZ = B

] = C

0 = D

22 = E

< = F

" = G

99 = H

\ = I

1 = J

= K

@ = L

+ = M

x = N

! = O

$ = P

^ = Q

& = R

: = S

4 = T

K = U

33 = V

= = W

? = X

() = Y

* = Z

JOKE BREAK

What do you call five identical Harleys?

Quints.

Why did Cheetah and Beast Boy run outside?

They heard it was raining cats and dogs!

A **pun** is a joke that uses words with multiple meanings. For example, a mug is a type of cup, but *mug* can also mean to steal something from someone.

Try to come up with your own puns—just remember that nobody is *pun*nier than Harley Quinn!

Weird but True!

Did you know that cats have two sets of vocal cords? It's true! One is for meowin', the other's for purrin'.

What does Frost say when she wants people to calm down?

"Everybody chill!"

You laughed, didn't you?

That's funny, because I was *Harley* jokin'.

Only two more riddles to go! Can you figure out Clue #4?

Dear Harley,

It's flat, broad, and vast.
It waves but doesn't see.
Some might call it the ocean,
But I call it the _____.

—A Friend in the Know

ANSWER: Sea.

For KICKS and GiGGLES

What did Cheetah say when she found out she wasn't named Hero of the Month?

"This is a *cat*-astrophe."

What does Cheetah do when she needs to re-energize?

She takes a quick *cat*-nap!

Why shouldn't I tell jokes about Cheetah and Catwoman anymore?

It hurts their *felines*.

LAST LAUGHS

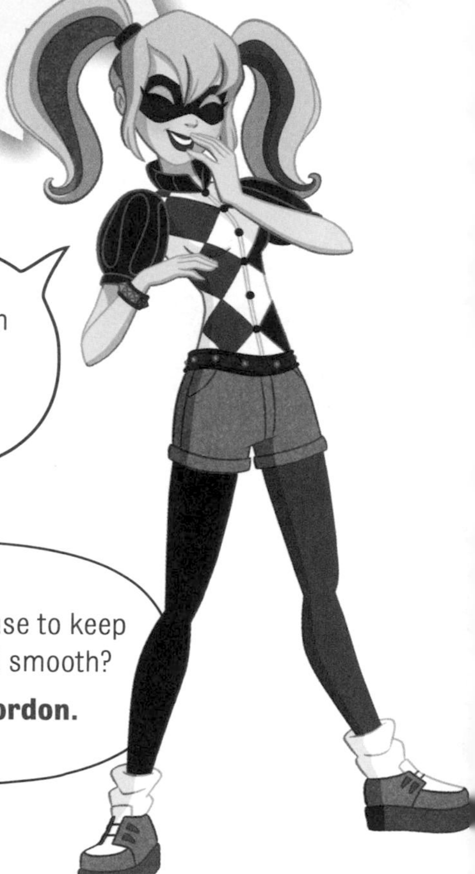

Why does Barbara Gordon love baseball?

She's a *Bat*girl!

What does Batgirl use to keep her hair silky and smooth?

***Conditioner* Gordon.**

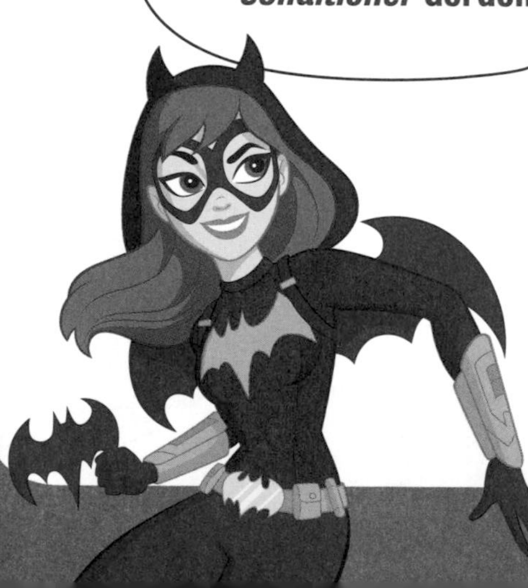

Supergirl is technically an alien, but did you know she likes life on Earth?

Apparently, outer space is kinda boring. No atmosphere.

How do villains prefer to confront Wonder Woman?

From far away!

Name _____ Date _____

All right, junior jokesters, you've had plenty of practice using ciphers and breaking codes. Now it's time to put your skills to the test. Pick your favorite form of encryption—everybody's got one, right?—and write a secret message to a friend. Use the space below to practice. When you're ready to pass the note, make sure your friend has the key to crack the code; otherwise they'll be reading gibberish all day!

RIDDLE ME THIS

Finally! It's the last clue. We're so close to figurin'
out who's coming to Super Hero High!

Dear Harley,

You've solved four of my riddles.
I'll give you the fifth one for free.
The last clue is **H**.
Who could this new teacher be?
—A Friend in the Know

LET'S USE OUR *NOGGINS*

Hey, Harley fans!

Did you solve all the riddles? Let's put the answers together and take a look at the clues.

Pea

The letter *S*

Why

Sea

The letter *H*

Hmm . . . what do these answers have in common?

Looks to me like *pea, why,* and *sea* could be letters, too. Maybe *pea* equals *P*?

Of course! Pea equals *P,* and *why* equals *Y.* Can you finish fillin' in the blanks?

P S Y __ __ !

RIDDLE ME THIS

We got another note from our mysterious messenger!
Could this be a sixth clue?

Dear Harley,

You solved all my riddles,
But the result you might not like.
There is no new teacher,
And the answer is PSYCH!

Sorry, Harley. Turns out we won't be getting
a new teacher at Super Hero High any time
soon. It was only a rumor. I just couldn't
resist pranking the ultimate prankster!

—Your Friend and Fellow Joker,

Beast Boy

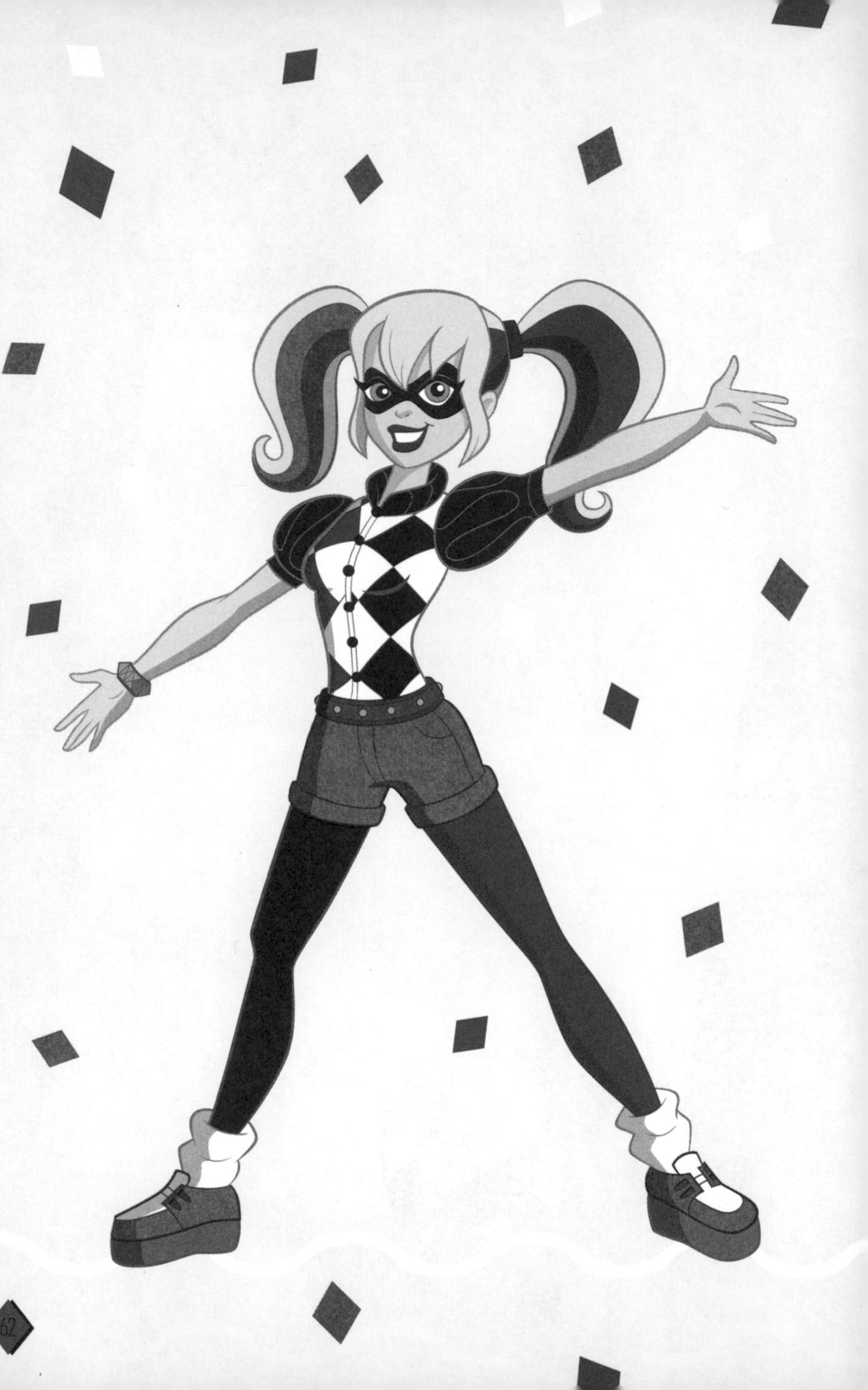

Wisecracking Beast Boy got me! Me! Harley Quinn! Nobody pranks this prankster!

I hope you'll help me figure out how we can turn the tables on this sneaky shape-shifter.

Until then, may your whoopee cushions be loud and your jokes be super.

—The One and Only

Harley Quinn